NURI MEANS LIGHT

By Joy E. Triche

Illustrations by Hamza "IN-ZO" Muhammad

Tiger Stripe Publishing
Chicago

Names: Triche, Joy. | Muhammad, Hamza, illustrator.
Title: Nuri Means Light / by Joy Triche; illustrated by Hamza Muhammad
Description: Chicago, IL: Tiger Stripe Publishing, 2019. | Summary: On her first day of school, a little girl explores the meaning of names.
Subjects: Identity ---Juvenile fiction | Personal Identity---Juvenile fiction
BISAC: JUV009080 JUVENILE FICTION/Concepts - Words
Identifiers: ISBN 978-0-9905895-7-0
27 26 25 24 23 22 21 20 19 18   1 2 3 4 5
First printing, May 2019

To KGB and JHB
Thank you for the gift of my name.

Greetings! I'm Nuri. You say it like this: *NOOr-ee*.

I'm starting school today. I wonder what I will learn on my first day. What do you think? Come on, let's find out.

"Welcome class! I'm your teacher Mr. Hoang (*HWÂNG*). When I point to you, tell us your name."

"My name is Mateo (*maht-TE-ō*)," shouts the boy in the yellow shirt.

Then the girl with the sandy-brown hair says, "My name is Brooklyn."

"My name is Rafiki (*rah-FEE-kee*). Rafiki means *friend*," says the boy in the blue shirt.

Hmm, does my name mean something? My name has to mean something. Doesn't it?

Oops! I missed some names, and now Mr. Hoang is pointing at me.

"My name is Nuri," I say in my strongest voice.

Do all names have a special meaning like Rafiki's?

"Does your name mean something?" I ask Barack (bah-RAHK).

He looks at me, a little confused.

"Like Rafiki, his name means *friend*, I say. "Does your name mean something?"

"Yes, Barack means *blessed.*"

"Blessed?" I ask.

"Yes. Like the way I feel when my Mommy hugs me tight," he says, smiling.

"Alba (*AHL-bah*) means *sunrise*. Daddy says that the sunrise is when the rays of the sun peek through my window in the morning," says Alba.

"The rays of the sun, huh? That's really cool," I say.

What could my name mean?

"My name is Shannon, and Shannon means *small* and *wise*," says the girl with the red hair. "My auntie says it describes me perfectly."

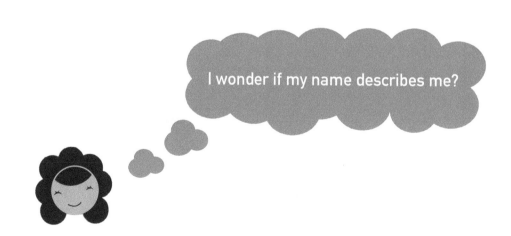

I wonder if my name describes me?

"My name is Misaki (*me-SAH-kee*). Misaki means *beautiful blossom*, like the roses in Grandma's garden."

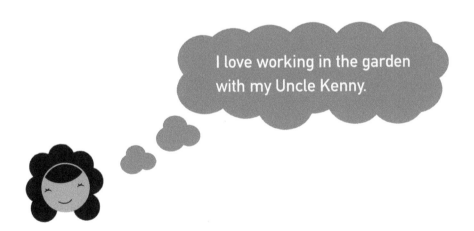

I love working in the garden with my Uncle Kenny.

"What does your name mean, Dayaal (*dī-AHL*)?" I whisper.

He looks up from his book. "Dayaal means *kind-hearted*," he whispers back.

"What's kind-hatter?" I ask a little too loudly.

"I said 'kind-**hearted**.' Like when my mom and I helped a baby bird back into its nest."

"What about you, Brooklyn? What does your name mean?"

"The Brooklyn Bridge is in New York City. It's where my mommy and daddy fell in love," she giggles. "They named me Brooklyn because they love me, too!"

"Well, Arthur is my dad's name and my grandpa's name, too," says Arthur. "I think it has to do with a king."

"What about you, Nuri? What does your name mean?" Zawadi (*zah-WAH-dee*) asks.

"I'm not sure, but I'm going to find out," I reply.

After school Mommy asks me, "what did you learn today?"

"I learned names have special meanings. My friends at school have names that mean things like *blessed* and *blossom* and *special helper*."

"Mommy, what does my name mean?"

"Nuri means Light," Mommy says.

"Light, like my nightlight?" I ask.

"Yes, it helps you see in the dark," says Mommy. "And Nuri means Light, like the Light God puts in each one of us. Light is special and very important—just like you."

At dinner we talked all about the special meanings of names, especially *my* name.

"My name is Nuri, and Nuri means Light.

What does your name mean?"

CPSIA information can be obtained
at www.ICGtesting.com
Printed in the USA
BVHW021734210519
548437BV00001B/1/P

9 780990 589570